Hello my friend!
Can you see the little white bungalow at the top of the hill?
There's someone **VERY** special inside.

To the people in the village Granny Norbag is just a lovely old lady who enjoys watching TV, knitting and playing bingo.

But Granny Norbag has a **BIG** secret. She owns a magical set of false teeth!

Granny Norbag and Engelbert found themselves on a small island surrounded by wate

Looking through her telescope, Granny Norbag spotted a large blue building in the distance.

LAND AHOY!

"Come on Engelbert! Land ahoy!" shouted Granny Norbag excitedly.

Inside the library Mabel the Mermaid told Granny Norbag how
Captain Oddsocks and his pirate crew had stolen all of the library books.

Granny Norbag made a pot of tea,
before bravely setting off to sort out those naughty pirates once and for all!

In a short while, Granny Norbag was rowing towards the scary pirate ship. "I have just the thing to get us on deck," she whispered to a nervous Engelbert.

Pulling a ladder from her handbag the plucky pensioner climbed on board, quickly followed by her feathered friend.

She dabbed them with her bingo dabber.

After a quick NANNA NAP and gossip over a cup of tea, with carrot cake, the pirates were exhausted.

Walking the wobbly wooden plank, Granny Norbag began to think of many things. First she wondered if she'd left the oven on, then if she'd put the bins out. Finally she asked, "Why aren't these rotten pirates reading the books that they've stolen?"

With a twinkle in her eye the brave pensioner asked for one last request.
"I want to read you a story!" she announced.

Soon the naughty pirates were
sat listening to a story
about a baby kangaroo.

THE KANGAROO
WHO COULDN'T JUMP

Granny Norbag gave the snotty crew [a] stern look until they remembere[d] their manner[s.]

Then, as Engelbert san[g,] she read story after stor[y] to Captain Oddsock and his gan[g.]

As the sun se[t,] the pirates to[ld] Granny Norbag tha[t] they stole the book[s] because the[y] could not read ther[e.]

A clever thought popped into Granny Norbag's head! "To the Mermaid Library!" she ordered. Soon after she was sharing her idea with a delighted Mabel.

From that day the library would become a school for pirates.

Mabel the Mermaid would teach the pirates how to read and write. In return they promised to behave and do all of their homework.

A delighted Captain Oddsocks promised Mabel that the next time
Granny Norbag visited the school, he would read her a story.

An alarm rang and Granny Norbag quickly picked up the television remote control.

EUCALYPTUS CREEK

"Eucalyptus Creek is about to start!" she announced with glee.

And this, my friend, is how our story ends.

As Granny Norbag and Engelbert sit down to watch their favourite TV show, with a nice cup of tea and a large slice of cherry cake!

'Bye for now!
See you in
our next
adventure!

In the meantime,
you can see more of what
Granny Norbag and Engelbert
are getting up to at:

 @grannynorbag

 @grannynorbag

 @grannynorbagbooks

www.grannynorbag.co.uk

Join Granny Norbag and Engelbert in their next adventure
when they come across a scary Cave Troll....

...but, all is NOT what it seems!!